Contents

In Flanders fields the poppies blow

Between the crosses, row on row

    That mark our place; and in the sky

    The larks, still bravely singing, fly

Scarce heard amid the guns below.

We are the Dead. Short days ago

We lived, felt dawn, saw sunset glow,

    Loved and were loved, and now we lie

    In Flanders fields.

from 'In Flanders Fields'

John McRae 1915

Stephen Potts

TOMMY TROUBLE

Illustrated by Stephen Player

mammoth

For Rosemary
Stephen Potts

To Danny
Stephen Player

First published in Great Britain in 2000
by Mammoth, an imprint of Egmont Children's Books Limited,
a division of Egmont Holding Limited,
239 Kensington High Street, London, W8 6SA

Text copyright © 2000 Stephen Potts
Illustrations copyright © 2000 Stephen Player

The moral rights of the author and illustrator have been asserted

ISBN 0 7497 3952 5

10 9 8 7 6 5 4 3 2 1

A CIP catalogue record for this book is
available from the British Library

Printed in Great Britain by Cox & Wyman Ltd,
Reading, Berkshire

1 Craaark!

Tommy Cameron lay awake, waiting. He watched the curtain shadows fade, and the wall between them pinken as another sun struggled skywards. Tommy listened hard for steps in the street below. There'd been no post from Dad for ages. *Maybe today*, he thought.

There was a stirring in the cot beside him. The postman's familiar knock at the downstairs door snapped the baby's eyes open.

'Don't cry, Aileen,' Tommy whispered.

'Please don't cry.' He listened as he stroked her silky hair, trying to smooth away her gathering frown.

The knocking came again, and his mother's voice rang out in reply, 'All right, all right, I'm coming.'

Aileen began to bubble at the din. Tommy scooped her from the cot and swung her gently in his arms, murmuring shushes the while. It didn't work: her cries grew louder.

Tommy heard the postman's farewell below, then steps on the stairs. His bedroom door swung open and there stood his mother in her blue dressing-gown, looking tired again. Where he clutched a wailing baby, she held a heavy package and some letters. They swopped burdens. The package was just another catalogue, and all the envelopes were printed and official looking. None of the writing was Dad's. It had been so long since he'd sent anything. One by one, Tommy held up the letters, still half hoping.

'Scottish Gas,' sighed his mother. 'Scottish Power. British Telecom.' The baby was quieter now. 'I know. Nothing but bills, eh, son?' Tommy looked at her in the low light. She looked away, and fumbled with her free hand in her dressing-gown pocket. She held up an empty red-and-white cigarette packet, and smiled sadly at him. 'Tommy, would you . . .?'

He stared back. The pack had been full when he went to bed. His mother, not smiling now, slid some coins on to the catalogue he cradled. 'Two packets, on your way home from school.' She swept past him to her own room, Aileen asleep once more on her shoulder.

Tommy washed, dressed and descended to the kitchen. He rummaged in the cupboards for cornflakes and shook out a bowlful, before he saw the milk had run out again. He opted instead for toast and jam and was on his second slice when his mother called down, 'Tommy, watch the time. Don't be late again!'

He peered at his Mickey Mouse wristwatch, frowning, then at the clock on the cooker, the one with numbers. She was right: he had ten minutes. Muffling his goodbyes with the last of the toast, he stuffed a handful of dry cornflakes into the pocket of his black school jacket, and ran out.

It was hard to run with a mouthful of toast, so he slowed to a walk as he passed the war memorial on the green. Overhead, crows swirled in the wind-riven treetops and called raucously. Late though he was, Tommy sat on the stone steps to watch a while. Once he'd got his breath back he set off again, this time with his jacket hitched over his head, and his arms spread wide. He tried a crow call. 'Craaark.' Nothing happened. He bent his knees, hopping ahead with his feet together and his head tucked in, and called again, louder and harsher this time: 'Craaark!' Some crows looked down, but only for a moment. Tommy hitched his jacket higher still, and flapped his outstretched arms, black-gloved fingers splayed like wing-end feathers. His awkward crow-hop turned into a run, straight ahead at first, then wheeling left and right in ever-tighter circles. He slalomed along the avenue of trees, a cornflake spiral spraying out behind him like golden snow. 'CRAAAAARK!' he yelled at the top of his voice, over and over. When at last he stopped to look up, breathless once more, there was silence overhead. He smiled.

Tommy felt suddenly embarrassed. Maybe people, as well as crows, had witnessed his performance. He straightened up and looked around. No one. Relieved, he headed off for the torment of another day at school, crunching cornflakes underfoot.

2 'What's the trouble, Tommy?'

Mr Sutherland's voice droned on at the front of the class, while Tommy gazed out of the window near the back. There wasn't much to see. He turned back to the classroom, looking over the rows of desks in front of him to the blackboard, where the squiggles made no more sense than usual. Tommy knew he should concentrate, but he couldn't. He stared at the long line of marks on the top of his jotter – one for each day his dad had been gone – and sadly added another.

'Remembrance Day began after the First

World War.' Mr Sutherland squiggled on the blackboard as he spoke. 'They called it the war to end all wars, but twenty-one years later there was another one, even bigger. The Second World War. On Sunday we remember both of them. This is one of the most famous poems from the first – the Great War. I'd like you to copy it into your jotters.'

Tommy grasped his pencil tight, his tongue between his teeth, and set to work as the teacher prowled about. Bent ever closer over his book, he felt Mr Sutherland approach from behind, the creeping shadow of a growling cloud.

'What's all this, Thomas Cameron?' Mr Sutherland asked, sliding the jotter off the desk. Tommy's paralysed pencil left a thick grey line on the page, like a smoke trail from a plane about to crash. Tommy stiffened: whenever a teacher used his full name, it spelt trouble. Mr Sutherland read from the board:

> In Flanders fields the poppies blow
> Between the crosses, row on row

And then from Tommy's jotter:

> Tommy Gameron, Tommy Cameron.
> ~~To Tommy~~ Tommy Cameron.
> Tommy Cameron, Tommy Cameron.
> Tommy Cameron, Tom

Tommy winced. Nearby classmates nudged each other into titters.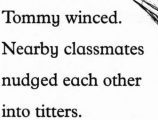

Mr Sutherland flicked back through the pages to yesterday's lesson, and beyond. 'Tommy Cameron. Tommy Cameron. Tommy Cameron,' he read again.

He put the jotter down with a sigh. Tommy stared hard at the desk top. 'What's the trouble, Tommy? Can't write? Can't read? Or just can't be bothered?' Some children now laughed out loud. Tommy didn't need to look up: he knew their voices. 'See me afterwards, Tommy,' Mr Sutherland said firmly, then moved on down the line of desks.

At home-time, several children waited for him outside the school gates, and fell in behind as Tommy hurried home. 'What's the trouble, Tommy?' they mocked, over and over. Mr Sutherland's stern words after class still rang so loudly in his ears that Tommy didn't notice at first. Then he tried to ignore them, walking faster and faster as the laughter loudened. Soon he was running. He didn't notice the coins spilling from his trouser pockets, but the chasing children did. Some stopped to fight over this unexpected booty.

Tommy ran under the trees. He stopped to grab the biggest stick he could see, and raced for the sanctuary of the memorial steps, where he turned to brandish his wooden sword. He didn't say anything, but his pursuers knew from his face not to go nearer. They lobbed a few stones, still jeering, 'What's the trouble, Tommy?' till old  Mrs McSorley across the street banged angrily on her window and they all ran off.

When he was sure they had gone, Tommy dropped his stick, slumped against the rough cold stone, and finally gave way to the tears he had fought off all day. He didn't cry for long, and as his sobs subsided his fingers traced the lettering cut into his stone shelter. He suddenly stopped, looking at one set of letters in wide-eyed surprise. As he stood up to investigate further, a five pence piece clinked to the floor. Tommy patted his pockets in rising panic. His mother's cigarette money was gone.

He ran to the shop on the corner, turning over in his head the best way to put his question. Nothing sounded right, and once inside the shop he simply froze, staring wordlessly at the man behind the counter.

'Well, lad?' barked the shopkeeper, staring back. 'Out with it.'

'C-cigarettes, for Mum, please. Her usual. Only I haven't the money. It all fell out when they chased me. I can get my pocket money from home, but I have to take the cigarettes there first. Please, mister.'

The shopkeeper shook his head. 'What

do you think this is, lad? A charity? Your ma's way behind already, and I'm blowed if I'll start a tab for *you*.' Tommy heard the door, and sensed someone come in behind him. The shopkeeper's eyes flicked up for a moment, then back down. 'Now off with you. You know fine well I shouldn't sell them to you at all. You're way under age.'

Tommy turned away. His path to the door was blocked by an older boy, Davey. Tommy was wary of the way he slouched around – alone, unwashed, silent – and stepped back to let him pass, not meeting his eye. Davey and the shopkeeper waited, saying nothing till Tommy was outside, but through the window he saw the shopkeeper's hand reach along the cigarette shelves to the Regal King Size.

Back at the war memorial, Tommy pondered. Maybe he should go straight home: he was already late. But to turn up cigarette-less . . . She'd be angry either way. Unable to choose, he did nothing but shiver as the daylight dimmed and the fallen leaves blew round his feet.

He watched as Mrs McSorley emerged from her front door, like a mole from its burrow, in her black coat and hat and gloves. The plastic bags she held filled with sudden wind, flapping loudly as she stopped by the postbox to slip in a letter, before shuffling on to the shops.

It was nearly dark, and beginning to rain when she returned, bags bulging. Noticing

Tommy as she opened her garden gate, she paused, lowered her shopping on to the doorstep, and crossed the street to him.

'Timmy, isn't it?' she asked. He was too cold to correct her. 'What's the trouble?'

Tommy winced – those words again – but he could see she meant it kindly. He explained about the money. She pulled out her purse. 'I saw them chase you, right enough, son.' She held out some coins. 'Here, Timmy. There's enough for one pack, if that's what it takes for you to go home to the warm. Your ma won't want you sitting here to catch your death, now, will she?'

Tommy hesitated, till her smile told him it really was all right. He teeth-chattered his thank you and raced to the corner shop. He had to hurry now.

When he saw the money in Tommy's hand, the shopkeeper seemed to forget he was under age and served him in sullen silence. Tommy was soon panting on his own doorstep, with the precious packet in his pocket. His mother answered the door, and Tommy held his breath. She pulled him to her and puffed it out of him in a big hug.

'Oh, Tommy where have you *been*?' She closed the door and swept him into the kitchen where Aileen gurgled in her highchair, her chin plastered with baby food. 'You're cold and wet and I was so worried about you.'

Tommy placed his red-and-white trophy on the table. 'I could only get one because I lost the money,' he said.

'Is that why you're so late?' his mother asked. 'You were frightened to come home?'

Tommy nodded. His mother went quiet and looked away at the rain pattering the windowpanes. When she looked back, her eyes were glistening. 'You must be hungry,' she said. 'Come on. Dinner's ready.' It was only when she mentioned it that Tommy realised he was starving.

3 Remembrance Day

Saturday spelt freedom from lessons and, when the sun shone as it did today, Tommy just had to be outside. The crows weren't at home but, strolling in the grass beneath their trees, Tommy found an old tennis ball. It was still full of bounce but too slimy with dog slobber to hold. Tommy flipped it from foot to foot, then kicked it idly at a nearby tree trunk, and neatly trapped the rebound. Other trees crowded in: they wanted the ball back. 'Right,' said Tommy, and he set off, dribbling the ball past tree after tree, skipping over their outstretched roots. The crowd's roar loudened as he played a slick one-two with a wooden bench before rounding the last line of tree defence and looping the ball over the goalkeeper bush into a litter bin. The crowd went wild and even some of the trees applauded.

Tommy celebrated, copying the players at the matches Dad used to take him to, then bent over the bin to retrieve his ball, hoping the dog slobber was gone. A car stopped across the road, outside Mrs McSorley's house. Tommy stood up, embarrassed. The crowd was quiet now.

The car had a light on its roof with letter-squiggles on it. The first was a T, and one of the others was an X. An old man rose stiffly from the back seat as the driver hauled a battered green suitcase from the boot. The man caught Tommy's eye as he swopped the suitcase for some money. 'Some goal, that, lad,' he said. Tommy blushed beetroot, but the man didn't see, for Mrs McSorley had flung open her door and was calling to him.

'Jack!' she shouted, beaming broadly as she ushered him in.

The next day Tommy mooched about the kitchen as he usually did on Sunday mornings. 'Away out from under my feet, Tommy,' said his mother as she loaded the washing-machine. 'Why not find your wee friends from school, mmmmm? Jumper on and off you go.'

Once outside, Tommy dawdled aimlessly along the lines of parked cars, trying to whistle. On Sundays past, Dad would take him fishing, or share a kickabout on the green. Now his mum seemed to think he had friends who would do the same. Didn't she notice?

Without planning it that way, he found himself drawn to the war memorial. All around it clustered sombre-looking people watching the minister from the church. He stood on the lowest step with a big black book in one hand and, in the other, a small white handkerchief into which he blew loudly. So *this* was what Mr Sutherland had been on about.

At the back of the group fidgeted band boys, with battered brass instruments hung

round their necks. On either side were little knots of local people, some watching the minister, but most inspecting the neat rows of old men in the centre of the gathering, standing stiff backed and smart in poppy-splashed black. Some wore strange soft hats Tommy hadn't seen before, and most had shiny tokens dangling from bright ribbons on their coats. Among them was

Jack, clutching a ring of red flowers.

'They shall grow not old as we who are left grow old,' snuffled the minister.

Tommy found it hard to make sense of what he said. He crept closer to listen and to watch.

Most of the men had bowed their heads but Jack was looking up. Tommy followed his gaze to the stone cross atop the monument, now burnished gold by the low sun. Jack stared at it so intently Tommy felt he must be seeing something else as well, something far away and long ago.

'Age shall not weary them, nor the years condemn,' the minister droned. Tommy watched Jack's gaze drop from the cross to the black squiggles cut into the stone below it. His eyes moved slowly from side to side to scan the writing, with pauses here and there, while his lips moved soundlessly.

The minister stopped and there was a sudden silence. A whispering boy at the back was angrily shushed by the bandmaster. Jack stepped forward, his white hair lifted by a waft of wind. The tokens on his chest chinked as he bent to lay his plate of flowers on the middle step. He straightened and stepped back, staring at the marks in the stone above it. Tommy stared too, at one set of squiggles in particular.

'At the going down of the sun, and in the morning, we will remember them,' said the minister.

Jack, the other old men, the band, and the villagers all joined in. 'We will remember them,' they said.

Afterwards, when everyone had gone, Tommy sat on the steps for a long time, until the sun dipped behind the trees and it began to get dark. Lights flickered on in the old lady's house opposite. He saw two shadows, side by side, each drawing a curtain across. The larger shadow – Jack –

paused a moment, looking across at Tommy. Then the curtains closed, the light was gone, and Tommy was left with his thoughts once more.

'At the going down of the sun . . .' the man had said '. . . we will remember them.'

But here he was, on his own, unremembered, he felt, by anyone. And what about Dad? Had he forgotten too?

4 'Call me Jack'

Tommy meandered home from school, not chased today, and free to take his satchel-swinging time. Near the shop Davey slouched against the wall, smoking. Davey took his cigarette from his mouth, as if to speak, as Tommy drew near. Tommy looked away and hurried on by. Davey shrugged and took another puff, blowing smoke after Tommy's departing shoulders.

Tommy was so caught up with wondering what Davey wanted that he didn't notice the figure on the war memorial steps until it spoke to him.

'All right, lad?' Jack said, warmly. Tommy stopped, all thoughts of Davey away. Jack shifted along and moved some of the plates of red flowers to make room. 'Taken your seat, have I? Here.' Tommy clutched his satchel but didn't sit or speak.

Jack nodded at the battered school bag in Tommy's grasp. The initials on it had almost worn away. 'I hate homework too,' he said. 'Much rather play football.' Still Tommy said nothing. Jack pointed to the trees over Tommy's shoulder. 'Or conkers. D'you reckon there's any left?'

Tommy frowned. 'What's conkers?' he asked.

Jack stood up. 'We'll need sticks,' he said. 'Seen any about?'

Tommy's curiosity overwhelmed his doubts. 'Over there,' he pointed. 'Behind that tree. I left one there in case I needed it.'

Jack stopped himself asking what need Tommy might have for a stick, and followed him over. Tommy put down his bag, picked up his former sword, and handed it to Jack.

'Mmm,' said Jack, craning his neck to look aloft. 'One or two at best.' He took careful aim and hurled the stick high into the chestnut tree's branches spreading overhead. The stick disappeared briefly from view before tumbling back down, followed by a few leaves which twirled gracefully earthwards. 'Your turn,' said Jack.

Jack and Tommy alternated throws, Jack's being generally higher and more accurate, at least until he tired; but none was fruitful, and Tommy grew frustrated and careless. He hurried one throw, before Jack was ready, and the stick slipped from his hand into a wayward arc well off target and over Jack's head. 'Look out, mister!' Tommy yelled.

Jack ducked, his hands clasped over his head, and the stick crashed to the ground by his feet, followed by a patter of tree debris.

Tommy froze, fearful of Jack's anger, and watched as the old man slowly straightened.

'Jack,' he said, simply. 'You can call me Jack. And you are?'

Tommy let out his hard-held breath. 'Tommy. Tommy Cameron.'

Jack held out a big rough hand. 'Pleased to meet you, Tommy Cameron,' he grinned. 'TC, eh? So those aren't your initials on the bag there?'

Tommy looked down a moment, then shook his head. 'Dad's,' he said. 'It used to be his.'

'Passed down the family? I like that.' Jack was looking at the ground. He'd spotted something. 'Now, Tommy Cameron, by rights I should chide you to mind where you fling that stick.' Jack pushed aside the grass with his foot to reveal a freshly landed conker capsule, all soft, green and spiky. 'But looking at this, I'm not so sure. Well done, lad.'

5 Paper poppies

Each day after school, for as long as the sunshine lasted, Tommy met Jack by the memorial for conker contests. Tommy usually won, but wondered if Jack was letting him. By Thursday there was rain again, and Tommy puddle-splashed up to the memorial, not really expecting Jack to be there, but still disappointed he wasn't. The flowers he'd laid drooped wetly, flattened like bloodstains on the stone steps. It didn't seem right. He picked up the plate Jack had laid. It was heavy with wet. The ink on the label had run in the rain, and dripped blue-black through his fingers as he tried to make sense of the squiggles.

Later, while his mum was cooking tea, Tommy ran another cigarette mission to the shop, under fire from relentless rain but tempted by the promise that he could spend the change on sweets. He was so intent on choosing between Whizz-Bangs and Sherbet Shells, that he didn't notice Jack come in until he heard his voice on the other side of the shelves. Something in his tone made Tommy not want to be noticed, so he crouched low behind ramparts of newspaper and chocolate, listening.

'I can't believe it,' declared Jack, jerking a thumb towards the war memorial, whose steps Tommy knew were now bare of flowers. 'Not four days they lasted. Such hooligans, young people today. They've no respect.'

The shopkeeper nodded. 'Kids, eh? You ask me, I blame the parents.'

Tommy made himself small and still and silent until Jack left. Jack's anger told him it had all gone wrong, though he didn't understand how. Maybe if he rushed back there was still time, before his mum got angry too. He forgot about the Whizz-Bangs and the Sherbet Shells, and even about the change, and hurtled homewards.

He stood on his doorstep a while, heart a-hammer, then swung the door open and stepped into the kitchen. She wasn't there, and for a moment he thought there was still a chance. Then came her footfalls, heavy on the stair. She struggled into the kitchen under a dripping pile of flowers which she laid amid the clutter on the table. Her face was tight with anger and her effort to suppress it.

'Well?' she asked in a controlled voice that worried him.

'I'm sorry,' was all he could say.

'*Why*, Tommy? What did you bring them home for?' Louder, angrier.

'I've never had flowers before –'

'They are *not* flowers and they are *not* yours!' She was shouting now. 'They are wreaths, and they're meant to stay where they were left.'

'But – but – but the man with the book said they're for me,' blurted Tommy, close to tears. 'Me and the others with our names up there.'

His mother shook her head. 'Enough, Tommy. No more of your nonsense. You're to take them back right now.'

Tommy hesitated, staring at the wreaths, then at his mother, then back at the wreaths. He didn't understand.

Seeing this, his mother softened. 'They're not for you,' she said, as she bent down to him. 'They're for people who've gone, son.'

Tommy gathered up all the wreaths he could carry, and looked up at her. 'People who've gone? Like Dad?' he asked.

His mother said nothing. She piled up the rest of the wreaths and followed him out of the door.

Idling home from school the next day, Tommy approached the war memorial. Jack sat on the steps as before, flanked by the replaced wreaths. 'Hello,' he smiled.

Tommy paused, and half smiled back. 'I can't stop,' he said, edging away. 'I'm to go straight home. Ma said.'

Jack looked from the wreaths to Tommy.

'Tommy? Did you . . .?' The rest of the question was a gesture.

Tommy stopped backing off and when his reply came it was almost shouted. 'They were *my* flowers! *He* said so. You were *there*. "They shall not grow mould", he said.' Tommy paused, then resumed more quietly. 'It was raining. I wanted to look after them.'

At first Jack was taken aback, but then he began to laugh, softly at first, then louder and louder. He stopped abruptly when he saw Tommy's face. People were always laughing at Tommy. It always hurt.

'I'm sorry, lad,' soothed Jack. 'Will you . . . will you come and have tea with my sister and me? I'll square it with your ma.'

Tommy nodded agreement, and went

with Jack to tell his mother. While she and Jack talked on the doorstep he raced upstairs and dug out the battered metal tin where he kept his pocket money.

On the way to Mrs McSorley's he measured out the cost of a packet of cigarettes – it seemed so much – and handed it to Jack. 'Will you give this to her for me? I owe her. For cigarettes.'

'Oh?' Jack's eyes widened in surprise, till Tommy explained. 'Why not give it to her yourself?' he asked.

'Because I want you to tell her I'm not called Timmy.'

Jack paused, struck by Tommy's sudden firmness. His name *mattered*. 'Of course,' he said. 'And she's called Edna.'

An hour later, Tommy sat opposite Jack at Edna's kitchen table, scoffing his way through a pile of chips. Blood-red ketchup flecked his face. Jack was trying to explain about wreaths. '. . . so they're not real flowers. Paper poppies, that's all.'

Tommy nodded, but still didn't understand why grown-ups would lovingly string together pretty paper flowers into delicate red blooms, only to leave them outside in the rain. He didn't ask, for there was something else he needed to know.

'Why did you wear your money on your coat?' he asked.

'It's not money, lad. It cost a lot more than that,' said Jack, wistfully. He had the far-away look Tommy had seen at the war memorial.

Edna reached across to the mantelpiece and drew down a smart black box. She opened it carefully and showed it to Tommy. Inside, Tommy saw three heavy discs of different coloured metal, each with a circle of squiggles round somebody's head. Rainbow ribbons were carefully folded above each disc.

'No, Tommy, not money. It's medals. Now you can look, but not touch – not with those greasy chip fingers at any rate.'

Edna started to clear the table, ferrying dishes to the sink. 'Why don't you get on with your homework, Tommy, while we do these dishes. Then we'll all have a cup of tea and Jack here'll take you home.'

Tommy hesitated, then unslung his satchel from the back of his chair and slid out some books.

Jack cast sideways glances, in between his drying up. Tommy was certainly concentrating, but seemed to pay no heed to the textbook he'd opened at random in front of him. Jack returned a pile of plates to the dresser across the room, then peered over Tommy's shoulder. There were no words on the page, but Tommy was proudly applying the finishing touches to a drawing of the war memorial. It was only then that Jack noticed the textbook was upside down. He frowned, but said nothing, at least until they were out of the house, coats buttoned for cold.

'Tommy . . . you can't . . . reading's not easy for you, is it, Tommy?'

Tommy stiffened as Jack went on. 'Nor writing, neither?' Tommy shook his head, then walked on in silence till they passed the war memorial. A pointing arm shot up, and a high clear voice rang out.

'One nine one four. One nine one eight. I can do numbers.'

Jack stopped. 'Yes, Tommy, you can. And those are some special numbers you've just done. What about these, on this side?'

'One nine three nine. One nine four five.'

'That's right. Those numbers mean a lot to me. I'll tell you why one day. Now, let's be away home, shall we.' He lead Tommy past the darkened green, with its sentry-duty trees ever watchful.

Light streamed out from an uncurtained kitchen window in Tommy's house as they approached, while the neighbouring houses barely let loose a glimmer. 'It's like being an ARP,' said Jack as he knocked.

Tommy's mum opened the door and more light escaped. She didn't ask Jack in, but he could make out behind her the chaos in her kitchen. 'Here he is, Mrs Cameron, all fed and watered. Thanks for his company.'

'That's all right,' she replied.

'Only we didn't get much homework done, did we lad?'

'He never does.'

'You showed me how good you are with numbers though, eh, Tommy?'

'Oh?' she looked at Tommy, genuinely surprised.

Jack changed the subject. 'There were lots of Camerons round here, before the war. Would they be kin?' He was trying to figure something out.

Tommy's mum shook her head. 'It's a common enough name these parts, but no, we're from the Borders. And I was a Duffy before I got married. I've stayed a Cameron since . . .' Aileen started wailing within. 'Sorry – that's the bairn.

Come on, Tommy, off to bed with you.'

He exchanged waves with Jack as she ushered him into the kitchen and, as soon as the door closed, he asked her, 'What's an ARP?'

She bent to tend to Aileen and didn't look at him. 'No idea, Tommy. Never heard of it. Some kind of car?' She took the baby upstairs, where her cries slowly dwindled to silence.

Tommy sat by the fire, and watched the flickering flames. *Good with numbers*, Jack had said. No one had told him that before.

6 'It's not you, lad'

Tommy took careful aim and swung at Jack's conker. It broke into fragments which spattered the grassy ground at their feet. 'Two – nil,' he said with a grin. He liked this sort of number.

Jack cupped Tommy's conker in his hands, admiring its smooth woody beauty. 'It's a cracker, this one, Tommy. Usually the best lookers smash easiest.' He handed it back. 'My turn.'

Tommy held his prize nut at arm's length, not daring to look as Jack swung at it. Jack's striker again smashed into pieces. Jack whistled. 'When this season's done, lad, make sure you keep that one. Let it dry out slowly, mind: you'll have a killer conker next year. You'll beat all the other boys.'

Tommy had stopped grinning. He lowered his arm. 'Not you?' he asked.

Jack fumbled in his pocket for the last of his four conkers. 'I can't be sure when I'll visit again, Tommy. There's no saying how many winters I've left in me. Your turn.'

Tommy was stunned. 'Visit?' was all he could say.

'Yes, lad. Just the week. I'm away tomorrow.' Jack held out his conker arm.

Tommy swung furiously. Jack's conker shattered spectacularly and Tommy's flew out of his grasp and on to the flagstone floor of the memorial surround. Tommy turned and ran off, without a word. Jack watched him go, then stooped for the conker. He opened his mouth to call after Tommy, but held back when he felt a sharpness in his hand. He looked down. A harsh jagged

crack disfigured Tommy's treasure.

That night, Tommy lay in bed, lost in thought and not caring about conkers. First Dad, now Jack: who'd desert him next?

He heard something below his window: a hiss, then stifled sniggers. He got up to investigate and saw, in the street, a group of five or six boys, some of whom he thought he recognised. He watched them cross the road to the garden wall opposite. Two stood guard while the rest huddled round. There were more hisses and sniggers, then they all ran off towards the green. Under the street light, Tommy could make out a new squiggle on the wall. It made no more sense than all the other squiggles already there.

★　★　★

The next morning Tommy was despatched to the shop for some milk. First he crossed the road to the garden wall, where a new swirl of graffiti stood out sharply from the smudgy background. Tommy traced it with his fingers, then moved on, wondering what it meant.

As he approached the memorial he saw the same blue-black swirl newly daubed upon it, over and over. He broke into a run. *No*, he pleaded. *Not on my bit.* The closer he got the worse it looked. They'd painted it all. It was ridiculous to hope they might have spared one particular panel, or even a single name, but hope he did, until he ran round behind and saw it for himself.

He leapt up on to the step, patting his

pockets for something, anything, to take this polluting paint away. All he had was a Donald Duck handkerchief. He scrunched it into a ball and started rubbing furiously.

He didn't see the taxi pull up outside Edna's house, or hear it sound its horn. Edna opened her door and Jack emerged with his suitcase. On looking over, he signalled the taxi driver to wait, and crossed the road. Tommy, still unaware, concentrated his frantic scrubbing on one small patch of tainted stone, saying to himself, over and over, 'We *will* remember them. We *will* remember them.'

Jack squinted at the patch Tommy worked on. At the top of the panel, above vandal height, the stone still clearly declared,

'1914–1918. King's Own Scottish Borderers', but most of the names below were obscured by ugly sweeps of paint. The smudged patch where Tommy was working held just one name: 'Private Thomas Cameron'.

'It's not you, lad,' said Jack. 'It's someone else, a long time ago.'

Tommy ignored him and kept up both his scrubbing and his chant. 'We *will* remember them.'

The taxi horn sounded again. Edna stood by the open car door. She pointed at her watch.

'Tommy, I've got to go. Goodbye, son.'

Tommy dropped his inadequate cloth and turned to him. For the first time Jack saw the tears streaming down his face. 'Who is it?' he yelled. 'Who is it if it's not me?'

Jack had no answer. He shrugged and blustered and shook his head. 'I don't know, son.' Tommy was already scrubbing again.

'Tommy, I'll . . . I'll write, I promise.' Jack turned and hurried to the waiting car and his anxious sister beside it. As the car sped off, Tommy shouted after it, his voice cracked with anger and heartbreak.

'What good's that? Eh?'

Tommy was still scrubbing when Edna returned from the station, and most of the paint on his namesake had gone. Edna crossed over to speak to him, and winced when she saw his hands red raw, and the shreds of cloth at his feet.

'It's terrible what they've done, eh, Tommy? And that paint – so difficult to shift. You've done grand work on your wee patch, but all these other names . . . I don't know. See this one?' she pointed to another panel, a different name in a different regiment. Tommy finally gave up scrubbing and looked across. All he could see were straight black marks in stone, under swirly blue squiggles of paint. 'He was my uncle. Jack's uncle too, of course.'

The mention of Jack revived Tommy's anger, and cancelled out any curiosity he might have felt about Edna's uncle. He stepped down from his platform. 'I'm going home now, Mrs McSorley,' he said simply, and walked off.

7 Frozen out

In the days and weeks that followed, as winter tightened its frosty grip, Tommy trudged home each day from school, still half hoping to see Jack waiting for him on the memorial steps, and always saddened that he wasn't. He took scant comfort from seeing, in the daily-dimmer twilight, his own name standing out proudly from the paint-sprayed rest.

On a cold Saturday afternoon in early December, Tommy crunched frosted grass underfoot as he wandered across the green.

An impromptu football match was in full swing. Tommy stopped to watch. A classmate, Jimmy, was on the ball. His team-mates shouted at him to pass and his opponents at each other to tackle, but Jimmy ignored them alike, and moved in on goal, keeping the ball close, as if on an invisible string. The goalkeeper – Billy – lumbered out to meet him. Jimmy waited, then calmly stroked the ball between Billy's legs and the bag-and-coat goal posts. He turned away, arms spread wide, and lifted his jumper over his face like his TV heroes, as Billy's team-mates clustered round him. One of them, Kev, was angrier than the rest. 'For God's sake, Billy!' he yelled, puffing out clouds of vapour. 'You're a useless keeper!'

'I never asked to play in goal,' Billy sulked.

'You're even worse on the pitch,' said Kev, as he went off to recover the ball.

Tommy didn't notice Edna passing him on her way to the shops, till she spoke. 'Not joining in?' she asked.

Tommy didn't look at her. 'They don't let me play,' he said in a matter-of-fact way. He didn't want to watch any more, and headed away.

'What's the trouble, Tommy?' called Kev as he picked up the ball. All the other kids laughed, even Billy.

Tommy had to find somewhere else to mooch about. He couldn't stay indoors all day and he liked this tingle-fingered crunchy cold. He thought about the canal – perhaps frozen today. His mother and, before, his dad, had always warned him against going there alone, and he'd always obeyed. Until now.

Without really thinking about it he found his legs taking him to the edge of the village and across the fields, by the bridleway. He knew the route from the times his dad had taken him fishing. Mud ruts had frozen into ankle-turning ridges, and the water between them was frozen. Tommy jumped on every ice-mirror puddle he passed, till he reached the canal.

A bewildered swan sat on the bank, staring at the canal's stiffened surface. The ice looked thick and solid. Tommy lobbed stones of increasing size, but the ice didn't give. It took a large boulder, which he could hardly lift, to smash it, but then Tommy felt sad because it wasn't perfect any more. He picked up a chunk of ice with bubbles frozen in, and chucked it past the rubble he'd dropped on the surface.

It shattered into a thousand sparkly fragments, and the bigger ones skeetered along the ice for miles and miles, making a loud twangy noise which echoed for ages. He did this a few more times till he got bored, then stepped right to the edge and put a foot on the ice. He gently leant his weight on to it, feeling excited and scared in equal measure. He took a big breath, then swung his other foot down, but still held on to the bank. His heart was hammering now. He stepped out into the middle of the canal, not knowing why, and half waiting for a sudden crack beneath his feet and a rush of icy water round his legs.

'Hey!' Far along the towpath a man yelled at him. His big black dog barked and

ran towards Tommy, the man bustling after.

'Hey, laddie! Off of there! You'll go through!'

Tommy made for the bank, his footfalls heavier now. The ice groaned loudly, making Tommy move faster. Here came the dog. He dived for the edge as his left foot went through, but only to the ankle. He scrambled up the bank and over the hedge into the fields

beyond, bump-squelching his way to safety.
The man called off his dog and yelled after
him, but the only words Tommy could make
out over his own heavy breathing were, 'You
young tearaway!'

After the first field there was an old shed,
and Tommy leant against it to rest. To begin
with, his foot was too numb to feel cold, but

soon it began to hurt, so he took off his shoe and sock. He couldn't go home with them wet: his mum would guess and he'd really be for it. He wrung out his sock and hung it on a nail on the sunny side of the shed, then stuffed dead grass into his shoe and hung that up too. He took off one glove and put it on his foot, then sat back and waited.

When the sun dipped behind the hill, he put his shoe and sock back on. They were still wet, and steam came off them now his foot was warm. It mingled with his breath-clouds when he bent to tie his shoelace. It was getting dark quickly, though a big yellow moon hung overhead to light his way home. When he reached the war memorial, all daylight had gone from the

sky. Davey sat where Jack used to. He nodded as Tommy approached, and Tommy sat down too. Neither spoke.

Davey looked at the steam still rising from Tommy's shoe, then at Tommy. He took a big drag on his cigarette, then exhaled a cloud of smoke at the moon and offered his cigarette to Tommy. Tommy stared at the glowing red stick in Davey's fingers. A car swept by, its headlamps throwing giant boy-shaped shadows on to the stone behind them. Tommy looked round. In the moonlight he could make out just one name, the one he'd cleaned: his own. All the other names were so smeared with paint that everyone else would find them as hard to read as Tommy did. He glimpsed the name Edna had pointed out, and fell to wondering. Her uncle. Jack's uncle. Somebody's dad.

Tommy looked back at the cigarette in Davey's still-outstretched hand, then at Davey himself, blank eyed and silent. The memorial meant nothing to him, with or without graffiti, Tommy thought. Maybe he'd even helped spray it himself. Tommy looked Davey in the eye, shook his head firmly, stood up, and went home.

8 Hand to hand

It was cold again the next day too, with flurries of snow. Tommy put down the big old bucket, pressed the buzzer on Edna's front door, and waited, stamping his feet. Maybe he was too early. Edna opened the door in her housecoat, looking puzzled: no one called on a Sunday. Tommy smiled, tapped the bucket with a still-damp shoe, and asked brightly, 'Can I have some water? I've come to do your uncle.'

For a moment Edna was even more puzzled, until Tommy indicated the

war memorial with one hand, and then she understood. 'Of course,' she beamed, and took his bucket from him. 'You'll need a brush, and some soap, too.' She beckoned him to follow her into the kitchen.

She supplied him with warm water, made soapy with a big dab of washing-up liquid, and an old scrubbing brush with still-stiff bristles, then left him to it till the middle of the morning, checking through the window from time to time.

As the church clock chimed eleven, she ferried a tray across the street, laden with two steaming mugs of tea and a liberal supply of chocolate biscuits. She set it down on the lowest step, and stood back to admire Tommy's handiwork. He'd started by cleaning Thomas Cameron again, but was now scrubbing hard on the next panel. He broke off, apple-cheeked and puffing, to scoff a biscuit and slurp at his tea.

Edna sat down. 'I never met him,' she said. 'He was killed at Wipers, before I was born. But my old grandma went on about him so much I felt I knew him through and through. A fine man. Jack remembers him a bit.' She looked across the street, checking her open door. A small girl, younger than Tommy, watched curiously. Tommy didn't notice.

'What's an ARP?' he asked, spraying biscuit crumbs about when he said the P.

'Air Raid Precautions Warden,' Edna explained, as their tea went down. 'Someone who goes round houses at night, to make sure no light gets out for bombers to see. We don't have them now.' She emptied her mug and picked up the tray. 'It's a fair nipping day now, Tommy. Mind you don't get chilled.' She crossed back, and smiled at the girl as she passed. 'Hello, Kathleen,' she said. Kathleen smiled back, and carried on watching Tommy as Edna closed her door.

Before long there was another buzz at her door: Tommy again, with his bucket. 'More water, is it, lad?' she asked. He nodded.

'And another brush,' he said. Edna looked

across to the war memorial, where Kathleen was busy scrubbing away.

'Another brush. Of course,' she said. Tommy tried not to blush.

He trotted back across the road, a trail of spilt soap suds marking his path, and stepped up alongside Kathleen. They'd finished Edna's uncle, and had moved on to other names, taking a panel each, and scrubbing steadily. They were making progress when, out of nowhere, a football up-ended their bucket with a harsh metal clang, and soapy water washed round their feet.

Kathleen and Tommy turned to see five or six of the football boys glaring upwards at them. Kev bounced the ball menacingly. 'If it isn't the clean-up crew,' he sneered, then

volleyed the ball straight at Kathleen. Tommy tossed aside his brush and stepped in front of her to block the ball with his knee. It bounced high and fell to Billy at the edge of the gang. Kev laughed. 'C'mon, Billy, even you could hit a great big pile of stone.'

Stung by this, Billy tried to copy Kev's

kick, but muffed it, and spooned up a soft chip instead. Tommy trapped it easily, then kicked it straight back, hard. It hit Billy full in the face, and he dropped to the ground, shrieking. Kev looked at Jimmy, who raised his eyebrows, and collected the ball.

Tommy watched and waited. He hadn't meant to hurt Billy that much, but he knew they wouldn't believe him: some kind of revenge was surely coming. Jimmy placed the ball as if for a penalty, and took careful aim at the stone cross. No, Tommy thought. No you *don't*. Instinct took over when the kick came. Tommy stretched high above his head and leapt off the step. The ball hit one hand, and bounced up. Tommy's eyes never left it and, at the second attempt, he clutched it safely in both hands, just as he landed on the lower step.

He mounted the upper step, next to Kathleen, planted one foot on the ball and both hands on his hips, then looked from Jimmy to Kev. 'Who's next?' he said, surprising himself with his firmness.

Billy got up from the floor, still wailing, and backed off, as did the other kids, all except Jimmy. He spoke in a friendly tone Tommy had never heard from him before. 'It's OK, Tommy. I just wanted to see if you could do it again.'

Tommy picked up the ball, and bounced it two or three times. He looked at Kathleen. 'All right?' he asked. When he was sure that she was, he faced Jimmy again. 'What's the trouble, Jimmy?' he asked. 'Do you want your ball back?'

Jimmy grinned. 'Aye.' Tommy lobbed it gently up and Jimmy caught it. The danger to them over, the other kids crowded forward, led by Billy, who was angry, now that his wailing had stopped. Jimmy signalled to them to hold back. 'Leave him be.' He looked at Billy. 'We might need a goal keeper soon.'

Tommy watched them go, and only then did he notice how much he was shaking.

Kathleen stepped up beside him and gave him back his brush. 'You'll need this, Tommy,' she said. 'We've got work to do.'

For the rest of the morning they scrubbed side by side. Progress was slow, but as the paint cleared, Kathleen read out, one by one, the names they uncovered. Tommy traced the squiggles with his fingers, repeating each name after her, then hastening to uncover the next. In this way they worked through the alphabet, until there were just two names left, both beginning with W.

'Let's do these two together,' said Kathleen. They took a name each, rubbing resolutely with hands that were raw and arms that hurt. When at last they were done, Kathleen stood back. 'Private A.R. Williamson,' she read. 'And Private A.T. Williamson.'

Tommy repeated the names and stepped down beside her. 'I wonder if they were brothers,' he said.

The memorial gleamed golden in the low winter sun, sharp black names standing out proudly, like soldiers on parade. Crows swirled noisily overhead, bird bombers drawn by the lights which sparkled off the still-wet stone.

'Look,' said Tommy, pointing upwards. 'They like it.' Kathleen followed his gaze, staring long enough to get dizzy. A loud noise behind her made her jump, and she

turned to see Tommy running round the memorial with his arms outstretched, craarking loudly. She left the bucket on the steps to guard the memorial and followed, copying him as he raced off to circle the tree trunks, both of them breathless with craarking and laughter.

When they'd worn themselves out and it was time to take the bucket back, Tommy was surprised to see his mother chatting with Edna at her garden gate. She held something bulky and black in her hands.

'Hello, Tommy,' she smiled. 'Edna told me what you were up to. We're very impressed. Will you clean up your bedroom now, too?'

Everyone laughed, but this time Tommy didn't mind. He looked closely at the object she held, recognising it eventually as a camera. His mother held it up.

'I dug this out, to take a picture. It's . . . It used to be your dad's. He left it, along with some other stuff. I didn't like to touch it, but you've given me a reason. It's old but I think it still works. Come on.'

She started across the road, calling back. 'And you, Kathleen, bucket and all.' They trotted after her, and grinned broadly as she posed them either side of the bucket on the top step. Their handiwork shone behind them while she snapped away.

Edna served up tea for everybody afterwards, which they took outside in the last of the light. Tommy looked up at the stone cross. 'I wish Jack could see this,' he said, more to himself than to anyone else. Edna and his mother both heard him though, and they caught each other's eye. If Tommy had looked back as they took the tea things in, he would have seen his mother take Edna aside, for a quick but quiet question, followed by Edna's silent smiling nod. And if he'd not been waving goodbye to Kathleen when his mother took him home, he might have seen Edna slip a note into his mother's hand, the one he wasn't holding.

9 Private Thomas Cameron

Tommy Cameron lay awake, waiting. It was dark now when the postman came. He listened for footsteps, and watched the eastern sky pinkening as the midwinter sun struggled up to the horizon. There had been the odd Christmas card from a distant relative he'd never met, but nothing yet from Dad. *Maybe today*, he thought.

Aileen stirred in her cot. He stroked her thickening silky hair, and watched her as the doorbell went. She frowned, without opening her eyes, and when the doorbell went again she didn't respond at all. Downstairs he heard his mother. 'On my way,' she said. 'Just a moment.'

Tommy got up to investigate. He threw a dressing-gown over his too-small pyjamas, and went downstairs to the kitchen. The postie stood by the door, with a big brown-paper package in one hand and a heavy postman's bag slung over his shoulder. 'No, Mrs Cameron,' he said, pointing at Tommy. 'It says I've to get his signature too. Special request from the sender. Seems it's private.'

He put the package down on the table and thrust a clipboard and pencil at Tommy. 'Here, lad.' There was a paper with a mass of squiggles on it. He pointed. 'Your name, if you would, on the line, just there.'

Tommy looked at his mother, who nodded a puzzled approval. He signed his name and then, on impulse, added afterwards a word he'd practised on the war memorial steps after school: 'Private'.

The postman looked at the clipboard and laughed as he left. 'That's OK, son. I'm a captain, myself.'

Tommy's mum picked up the package and peered at the postmark. 'What's going on, Tommy? Who do you know over there?' Her pursed lips spread into a smile when she guessed the answer to her own question. She didn't tell him. 'Here you are, son. Why don't you open it?'

Tommy cut the string with the scissors she offered him, and ripped off the heavy brown

paper. Carefully wrapped within was a big
black leather-bound scrapbook. Embossed in
gold on the cover were words and numbers
only too well known to Tommy. He looked up
at his mother. '"Private Thomas Cameron",'
he read proudly. '"1896 to 1917".'

He opened the heavy cover, and flicked
through page after page of carefully
mounted pictures, cards, letters, newspaper
cuttings, and even, in the middle, a medal. A

loose note fluttered to the floor. Tommy picked it up and handed it to his mother. There was a catch in her voice as she read it out.

Dear Tommy,

When I left last month you asked who Private Thomas Cameron was and I didn't know. Seeing the picture your ma sent of you and Kathleen by the memorial made me want to find out. I've nearly lived in the library since, and I've tracked down his family, who've lent me some of this stuff.

Meet me at the usual place and I'll help you learn to read it all.

Love,
Jack

Tommy was gone. He shot through the still-open door like a greyhound after a rabbit, and hurtled along the street with his dressing-gown flapping behind him and his slippers flying off his feet. He raced past an astonished Kathleen, on the way to the shops with her mum. She turned to call after him: 'What's the trouble, Tommy?' but she could see from his crack-faced grin that there was no trouble at all. She watched as he raced away towards the memorial, where a waiting black-coated figure drew to his feet. Two sets of arms stretched out as Tommy raced towards him.

'Craark,' said Kathleen, under her breath, as she watched man and boy embrace. 'Craaaark.'